Skylark

Patricia MacLachlan

Illustrated by Elsie Lennox

Lions

An Imprint of HarperCollins*Publishers*

First published in the USA in 1994
by HarperCollins Publishers Inc.
First published in Great Britain in Lions in 1994
Lions is an imprint of HarperCollins Children's Books,
a division of HarperCollins Publishers Ltd, 77-85 Fulham Palace
Road, Hammersmith, London W6 8JP

3 5 7 9 10 8 6 4 2

ISBN 0 00 674952 X
[hb: 185600 6]

Printed and bound in Great Britain
by HarperCollins Manufacturing Ltd, Glasgow

This is for Emily MacLachlan –
with admiration
and love

Papa married Sarah on a summer day. There were no clouds in the sky, and Papa picked Sarah up in his arms and whirled her around and around, her white dress and veil surrounding them like the summer wind. Caleb was so excited and happy, he burst into tears.

Everybody was happy.

CHAPTER ONE

"Stand on that stump, Caleb. Anna, you next to him. That will be a good family picture."

Joshua, the photographer, looked through his big camera at us as we stood on the porch squinting in the sunlight. Caleb wore a white shirt, his hair combed slick to his head, Sarah in a white dress, Papa looking hot and uneasy in his suit. The lace at my neck itched in the summer heat. We had to be still for so long that Caleb began to whistle softly, making Papa smile.

Far off in the distance the dogs, Nick and Lottie, walked slowly through the dry prairie grass. They walked past the cow pond nearly empty of water, past the wagon, past the chickens in the yard. Nick saw us first, then Lottie, and they began to run. Caleb looked sideways at me as they jumped the fence and ran to us, running up to stand between Sarah and Papa as if they wanted to be in the picture, too. We tried not to laugh, but Sarah couldn't help it. She looked up at Papa and he smiled down at her. And Joshua took the picture of us all laughing, Papa smiling at Sarah.

Joshua laughed, too.

"Your aunts will like that picture," he said to Sarah.

Sarah fanned herself.

"They hardly know what I look like anymore," she said softly. "I hardly know what *they* look like anymore."

I looked at Caleb. I knew Caleb didn't like to think about Sarah and her aunts and her brother and the sea she had left behind.

"It's Maine you came from, isn't it?" said Joshua.

"Yes," said Sarah.

"She lives *here* now," said Caleb loudly.

Papa put his hand on Caleb's head.

"That she does," said Joshua, smiling.

He turned and looked out over the cornfield, the plants so dry they rattled in the wind.

"But I bet Maine is green," Joshua said in a low voice. He looked out over the land with a faraway look, as if her were somewhere else. "We sure could use rain. I remember a long time ago, you remember it, Jacob. The water dried up, the fields so dry that the leaves fell like dust. And then the winds came. My grandfather packed up his family and left."

"Did he come back?" asked Caleb.

Joshua turned.

"No," he said, "he never came back."

Joshua packed up the last of his things and got up in his wagon.

Papa looked at Sarah.

"It will rain," he said.

We watched the wagon go off down the road.

"It will rain," Papa repeated softly.

"Will you worry if it doesn't rain?" asked Caleb.

"Yes, but we'll get along," said Papa. "We always get along."

"Imagine having to *leave*," said Sarah.

Papa took off his jacket.

"We'd never leave, Sarah," he said.

"We were born here. Our names are

written in this land."

When Papa and Sarah went inside, Caleb looked at me. I knew what he was going to say, and I didn't want to hear it.

"Sarah wasn't born here," he said.

I picked up the pail of grain for the chickens.

"I know that, Caleb," I said crossly. "Papa knows it, too."

Caleb picked up a stick and bent down in the dirt. I watched him write SARA. He looked up at me.

"I'm writing Sarah's name in the land," he said.

"You can't even spell, Caleb," I said. "You can't."

I walked away. When I turned to look at Caleb, he was staring at me. I wanted to say I was sorry for being cross with him. But I didn't.

"Happily ever after," said Caleb when Papa married Sarah. "Now we'll live happily ever after. That's what the stories say."

Caleb said that all through the summer and the fall when the prairie grasses turned yellow, and through the first winter Sarah and Papa were married. He said it all winter long, when the wind blew around the corners of the house and ice sat slick on the windows. He said it when he fell into the slough and had to sit in a tub of warm water, his teeth chattering.

"I like the sound of it," Caleb told me. "Happily ever after."

CHAPTER TWO

The days grew hotter, the sun beating down on us. We stayed inside as much as we could. Even Nick and Lottie stayed inside, stretched out on the wood floor to keep cool. Papa walked the fields, measuring the level of the water in the well over and over, waiting for rain. He came in bringing the dirt with him.

"Papa!" I poked at his feet with my broom. "Your boots!"

I was sweeping, trying to keep the dust out. Sarah was scrubbing the kitchen floor on her hands and knees.

Papa was hot and tired.

"That may be the last washing for the floor," he said to Sarah. "We have to save water."

"That's a mixed blessing," Sarah said, brushing the hair off her face. She watched Caleb feed Seal.

"Don't feed her too much, Caleb," said Sarah. "She's getting fat with your food."

Papa looked closely at Seal. "I think she's more than fat, Sarah."

Sarah looked up. "What?"

"What does he mean?" asked Caleb.

I smiled.

"Kittens. He means kittens, Caleb," I said.

Caleb and I spoke at the same time.

"Can we keep them all?" I asked.

"When will she have them, Papa?" asked Caleb, excited.

"Don't know, Caleb," said Papa, drinking water from the tin cup. Sarah sat back.

"Has she ever had kittens before, Sarah?" asked Papa.

Sarah shook her head.

"No, never."

Papa smiled at Sarah's look. She stared at Seal for a long time.

"Kittens," she said, her face suddenly breaking into a smile. "Kittens!"

Late light fell across the bedroom, the windows closed to the prairie wind and the dust that sat on the windowsills and the furniture.

I held Sarah's wedding dress up to me and looked in the mirror.

"Anna?"

I jumped, startled, and Sarah smiled at me.

"I didn't mean to frighten you," she said.

I looked in the mirror again.

"Someday I'll marry and move to my husband's land. That's what Papa says."

"Oh he does, does he?" said Sarah.

"That's what you did, Sarah. You came from Maine to marry Papa," I told her.

Sarah was silent for a moment. She sat on the bed.

"Yes," she said slowly. "I guess I did."

"You fell in love with us," said Caleb in the doorway.

"I did that," she said. "First your letters. Then you."

"Did you fall in love with Papa's letters, too? Before you knew him?" asked Caleb.

I sat on the bed and watched Sarah's face as she remembered.

"Yes, I loved your Papa's letters," said

Sarah softly. "I loved what was between the lines most."

"What was between the lines?" Caleb asked.

Sarah looked at me when she answered.

"His life," she said simply. "That was what was between the lines."

"Papa's not always good with words," I said.

"Sometimes, yes," said Sarah, laughing. "But when I read your Papa's letters, I could see this farm, and the animals and the sky. And you. Sometimes, what people choose to write down on paper is more important than what they say."

Caleb didn't know what Sarah meant. But I knew. I wrote in my journal every night. And when I read what I had written, I could see myself there, clearer than when I looked in the mirror. I could see all of us: Papa, who couldn't always say the things he felt. Caleb, who said everything. And Sarah, who didn't know that she had changed us all.

Sarah loved the snow.

"We don't have drifts of snow in Maine," she said.

She waited and watched for it so she could paint the prairie snow with morning sun on it. She taught me to paint with watercolours, too. We painted the barn and tree by the cow pond, and we painted the sky just after sunset, Sarah's favourite time.

"When you can't tell where the colour comes from," Sarah said.

Chapter Three

On Sunday the air was still, the way it is before a storm. We dressed up and rode the wagon to church. Inside the church it was cool, like a prairie spring, and Caleb fell asleep. Matthew and Maggie, our closest neighbours, sat in front of us with their daughters, Rose and Violet. Tom, their baby, turned around and reached out to Sarah. She smiled and took his hand. Papa smiled, too. We all hated to go outside into the sun again.

Maggie and Sarah walked to the wagons, shading their eyes against the sun.

"Any news?" asked Maggie.

"Seal is having babies," said Caleb. "Lots of babies!"

Maggie laughed.

"That's big news. Come to think of it, I've seen Seal at our house," said Maggie.

"With Sam. The orange cat."

Sarah smiled.

"So it's Sam, is it?"

Sarah and Maggie laughed together. Then Sarah reached over and took Tom in her arms. She kissed the top of his head.

"I am surrounded by motherhood," she said softly.

I looked up at the way her voice sounded, sad and thoughtful. "A calf due soon," she added. "Then kittens."

Papa and Matthew came over, Papa's face serious.

"What is it?" asked Sarah. "What's the matter?"

"The church well is down. A whole foot," said Matthew.

"A foot!" exclaimed Maggie. "That's even more than ours."

Papa looked up at the sky.

"What if it doesn't rain?" asked Caleb.

I brushed his arm with my hand as if I were trying to brush away his words.

"It will rain, Caleb," I said.

Tom held out his arms to Papa, and Papa lifted him up, smiling.

"Are those clouds, Tom?" he said. "In

the west? Maybe it will rain. Maybe."

"Yes," said Maggie, trying to be cheerful. "It will rain." Her face looked thoughtful suddenly. "It *will* rain," she repeated. "It's just the time before it rains that is hard. It always is."

We rode home followed by clouds of dust tossed up by our wagon. The sky was blue. Heat waves rose off the land. As much as Papa wished for it, there were no clouds in the sky.

"Anna. Anna!"

I opened my eyes and morning sun poured across my quilt. Caleb was there, half dressed.

"What?"

"The calf is born. Hurry!"

Caleb pulled back my covers and I jumped up. We ran downstairs.

"Why didn't you wake us up?" I asked, excited. "When was he born?"

"She," said Papa. He sat at the kitchen table, drinking coffee. "Eat your breakfast first."

Papa drank coffee and Sarah put bowls on the table. Caleb tried to run out of the door, but Papa reached out and grabbed him.

"Eat," said Papa firmly.

"Hurry, Caleb! Eat faster," I said.

"I'm eating as fast as I can," said Caleb. "Is Mame excited? Does she like her baby?" he asked Papa.

Papa grinned at Sarah.

"An excited cow? I'm not sure I noticed. What do you think, Sarah?"

"I think she likes her calf," said Sarah, smiling back at Papa.

"What does she look like?" I asked.

"Small, brown," said Papa. "She has some white on her face."

Sarah looked at me over her cup.

"Your Papa says her face is as pale as the winter moon," she said. "And to think that you said that sometimes he is not good with words."

I smiled at Sarah.

"Moonbeam," said Caleb. "We could call her Moonbeam."

Papa laughed at the name.

"Finished," Caleb said, his spoon clattering in the empty bowl.

"Finished," I said.

And we ran out the door, where in the dark of the barn Mame looked up at us, her eyes steady. After a moment Mame leaned over to lick the calf that lay in the hay.

"Sarah's right," whispered Caleb. "Mame likes her calf."

Papa was right, too. Her face was as pale as the winter moon.

Sometimes Sarah dances, and she makes Papa dance, too, his face shy, his smile like Caleb's smile.

Sometimes, when Papa worries about the farm or the weather, Sarah takes his hand and pulls him outside.

"Come, Jacob, come walk with me," she says, smiling.

And he does.

They walk the fields and the country road, Lottie and Nick following them. Once they chased each other through the rows of corn and we could hear the sounds of their laughter.

CHAPTER FOUR

Papa came back from town with letters from Maine. Letters for all of us from Sarah's aunts: Harriet and Mattie and Lou. It was evening, the oil lamp shone bright in the kitchen. Papa mended a bridle, Caleb leaning against him. I read a letter out loud.

"'There was a storm,' Aunt Mattie says, 'and the porch shingles went to sea...'"

"What does that mean, went to sea?" asked Caleb, interrupting me.

"It means that they blew into the sea," said Sarah with a smile.

I began to read again. "'My hat went to sea, too. The one with the bird on it.'"

Caleb climbed up into Papa's lap.

"A real bird?" he exclaimed.

"Stuffed, Caleb," said Sarah. "Aunt Mattie will miss that hat."

"'Two inches of rain by the glass

measure...'"

I stopped reading, staring at the word rain. I looked up at Sarah, and she was watching Papa, her face touched by the light from the lamp.

"A glass?" asked Caleb.

I tried to make Caleb stop talking. I didn't want Papa to think about rain.

"What about your letter, Sarah?" said Papa.

Sarah shrugged.

"Just the weather," she said. "Painting William's boat."

Papa looked up at her.

"Read it, Sarah," he said softly.

Sarah took the letter out of her pocket. Slowly she opened it.

"'The grass is green,'" she read. "'Growing so tall that we've cut it dozens of times already. The trees are lush. Autumn will be beautiful. Come visit, all of you. Soon. Love, Mattie.'"

There was a silence in the room. Then Papa kissed Caleb and got up. He stood at the door, looking out at the red of the setting sun.

"It will be a beautiful sunset tonight," he said, his voice low. "I can tell."

Papa opened the door and went outside.

"A glass to measure rain?" asked Caleb again, still thinking of Mattie's letter.

"Hush, Caleb," I said.

Sarah didn't answer Caleb. She put her letter on the table, walked to the door, and went outside. I picked up the letter. There was more that Sarah hadn't read.

It has rained nearly every afternoon, Mattie had written. *It cools down the day and leaves us with good nights for sleeping.*

I watched Sarah put her hand on Papa's arm as he stood looking over the dry fields.

My eyes filled with tears.

I knew Sarah was sorry about the letters from Maine and the talk of rain.

It's not your fault that Maine is green, Sarah, I thought. *It isn't.*

It was dark and the moon was up when Caleb came in from outside, Nick with him. Sarah looked up from her book.

"Caleb! I thought you'd gone to bed long ago," she said.

"I had something to do," he said. "For Papa."

Sarah smiled and put her arm around him.

"Well, off to bed now. It's late. Both of you."

Caleb yawned and went up the stairs. Sarah got up and went out to the porch. Papa came across the yard from the barn, and he stopped suddenly, then looked at Sarah.

On the fence post was a small glass, sitting empty in the moonlight, waiting for rain.

Roses grew on the fence when Sarah came. And the fields were filled with wildflowers. I learned to float in the cow pond and Caleb ran with the sheep in the green fields.

Now clouds come and go, and the hot winds, too. But there is no rain for the roses. Dirt from the fields blows over everything, and the leaves have crumbled. "Like dust," Joshua said when he took our picture.

Like dust.

CHAPTER FIVE

Each day Papa dropped a rope with a stone down the well to measure the water level.

"Is it past the mark?" asked Sarah.

Papa nodded.

"How much, Jacob?"

Papa held out his hands a foot apart. Caleb and I got up into the wagon to go to town.

"Soon we'll have to haul water for the animals," said Papa.

"We can do that," said Sarah.

"We'll have to measure out our own water," said Papa as he climbed up.

"But we already do that, Jacob."

Papa looked down at Sarah.

"We'll have to use less."

Sarah stared at Papa, then got up to sit next to him.

"We can do that, too," she said firmly.

We drove off down the road. After a while Caleb poked his head between Sarah and Papa. Papa looked at him.

"So, Caleb?"

"*I* put the glass on the post," said Caleb.

Papa nodded but didn't say anything.

"To measure the rain when it comes," Caleb added.

"Thank you for that," said Papa.

"You're welcome," said Caleb happily.

He sat back in the wagon and folded his arms. Papa smiled.

All the way to town I looked for green. But as far as I could see the fields were brown. The wheat fields were dry. Turkey vultures circled in the distance. There was no green.

Everything seemed slow in town, as if the heat had taken over. Papa left the wagon in the shade of the granary and slowly unloaded his last bags of grain from the wagon. Slowly he walked inside.

Mrs Parkley's store was cool. Rose and Violet were there, Rose carrying Tom, who smiled at me. But Maggie had her arms around Caroline who was crying.

"Caroline? What's wrong, Maggie?" said Sarah.

"Their well is dry," Maggie said softly.

"Caroline," said Sarah. "What can we do?"

"There's nothing to do," Caroline said, drying her tears. "We've already packed up."

"Packed up!" said Sarah, shocked. "Where will you go?"

"They have family," said Maggie. Caroline took her packages and went to the door. She turned suddenly, her face sad.

"Joseph says we'll come back," she said. "But we won't. I know we won't."

She opened the door and left. Maggie walked over to the door and looked out.

"Surely we can do something," Sarah said. "We could haul water, Maggie. We could all work harder."

Sarah's voice grew louder, and Caleb moved closer to me.

"You can't just give up!" said Sarah. "You can't just give up everything you've worked for..."

Maggie whirled around, her face angry.

"You don't know how hard this is, Sarah," she said, angrily. "You haven't been in this kind of trouble before!"

Sarah stared at Maggie, then at the others in the store. Maggie reached over and took Sarah's hand. She opened the door and pulled her outside. I watched the two of them cross the dusty street. Maggie's arm went around Sarah, but they kept walking. Papa came out from the granary and watched them, too, Matthew beside him.

"Is Sarah angry?" asked Caleb.

I looked down at his worried face.

"No," I said. "Sarah's not angry."

Caleb sighed.

"Sarah likes to make things right," he said.

We watched without speaking, and then Joseph and Caroline's wagon passed, all packed with chairs and clothes and a cupboard, pots and pans tied on. Sarah turned to watch it, and Papa watched, too, from across the street. And then the wagon turned a corner and was gone.

Chapter Six

The ride home from town was quiet, the wind blowing dust around us.

"Any news in town?" asked Sarah wearily.

"Some news," said Papa. "Good news."

"Good news? What good news?"

"Your birthday is coming soon. Mattie wrote to remind me."

"She didn't!"

"She did," said Papa. "So—what do you want? Jewels, silk, travel?"

Sarah laughed.

"Travel? Where would I go?"

"Somewhere green," said Papa. "Somewhere cool."

Sarah looked at Papa.

"Do you think I would *leave*?" asked Sarah softly.

Papa was silent.

"Can we sing, Sarah?" asked Caleb.

"It's too hot, Caleb," she said. "Too hot for singing."

Papa flicked the reins over the horses' backs, but they wouldn't go faster.

"It's even too hot for Jack and Old Bess," he said.

I leaned back against the empty grain sacks and took out my journal, but it lay in my lap.

Caleb moved over close to me.

"Why aren't you writing?"

"There's nothing new to write," I said, lifting my hair off my neck. "There's nothing good. Just the heat. The fields are dried up. There's no rain."

"There will be rain," said Caleb. "Papa said so." He pointed. "That was the field where the wildflowers grew, remember, when Sarah came? The pond was full then. We went swimming and fell asleep in the grass."

I stared at Caleb, then out at the fields, remembering when the fields were green. Remembering when the days were cool. Remembering when Sarah came by train

and Caleb and I were afraid that she'd miss the sea.

Suddenly, Caleb stood up.

"Papa! Fire!"

In the west meadow a thread of smoke rose.

"Hold on," yelled Papa.

Sarah dropped to the wagon floor, and we held on as the horses raced for the yard.

Papa jumped down.

"Soak the grain sacks in the pond water! Hurry!"

Sarah and Papa ran to beat out the flames. We could see red flames in the dry grasses now. Caleb and I soaked the sacks, then ran closer to the fire, water dripping down our clothes.

"Stay back," warned Papa. "There's a wind coming up."

Nick and Lottie ran from the barn, barking.

And then suddenly Sarah screamed. Her skirt was on fire. Papa turned and threw Sarah to the ground and smothered the flames with a sack. He pulled her up.

"Are you all right?"

When Sarah nodded, Papa began to shout at her.

"I told you to stay back. You never listen! I *told* you there was wind!"

Caleb took my hand.

Sarah began beating the fire, now nearly out.

"You can't put out the fire alone!" she shouted. "Stop yelling at me!"

And then there was only smoke, the grasses all black and smouldering. Papa beat at one small flame. He stood back, and there was silence. Nick and Lottie stopped barking.

"We'll have to watch for fires all the time, now, even at night," said Papa, out of breath.

Sarah and Papa began walking back to the house. Sarah's hair was down; her clothes were wet and sooty. Papa looked at her, then away.

"You're a sight, you know," he said softly.

Sarah didn't answer.

Papa looked at her again, then smiled a small smile.

"You look...beautiful," he said.

I held my breath. I had never heard Papa say such a thing to Sarah.

Sarah kept on walking. Then she

turned and looked at him.

"Do you *really* think I would leave?" she said. "Just for somewhere cool? Somewhere *green*?"

This time Papa was silent. The two of them walked away from the blackened grass, past the dogs, and past us just as if we weren't there.

And that night, when Papa went out to close the barn door, Sarah ran after him. I saw them from my window. Papa took Sarah in his arms and kissed her, and they turned around and around and around, dust swirling over them in a cloud.

My dreams are cool. They are cool and the colour of the sky before rain, a dark and peaceful blue, the clouds edged in black before the rain comes and the earth smells sharp and sweet. I remember that smell.

The days are hot and still now.

Only my dreams are cool.

CHAPTER SEVEN

We sat on the porch out of the terrible sun, Maggie fanning herself, Sarah mixing batter for biscuits. Rose and Violet rolled a ball in the dirt to Tom. Caleb sat watching the sky for clouds.

"This heat," said Maggie wearily. "I dream of my old home sometimes. And I dream of long, cool mornings of sleep without the baby waking!"

Sarah smiled.

"Night dreams or daydreams?" she asked.

"What's a day dream?" asked Caleb.

Sarah sat back and looked at Tom crawling happily in the dirt.

"Sometimes, no matter where you are, you think of something sweet and cool. A place, maybe. And suddenly it's there. Or maybe it's something you wish for...and it is so near you can touch it, smell it...hear the sound of it..."

Sarah looked up suddenly as if caught up in her thoughts.

"She's dreaming about Maine," Caleb whispered to me.

No. *It's not Maine,* I thought. *It's not Maine she's thinking about. It's something else.*

Tom grabbed the ball and held it over his head. Sarah smiled.

"I have dreams, Sarah," Caleb said.

"Good dreams, Caleb?" she asked.

"I dream about rain," said Caleb. "Do you? Do you dream about rain?"

Sarah reached over and took Caleb on her lap.

"Yes, Caleb. I dream about rain."

"Good," he said. "Then it will come true."

But rain was only in our dreams. The winds came every day, blowing dust through the windows and into the house until it covered the furniture and got into the food and our clothes and hair. The land got even drier, and we stopped taking baths. Every day we hauled river water for the animals in big wooden barrels.

And then the worst thing happened.

We drove to the river in our wagon, empty barrels in the back. Clouds hung high in the sky. Maggie sat in her wagon by the riverbed. Matthew stood on the bluff over the river, looking down.

"Hello, Maggie," called Sarah.

But Maggie didn't speak. She didn't even look at us.

We got down from the wagon. The river was nearly dry, only a small trickle in the red prairie dirt.

Everyone was quiet.

"What will we do?" whispered Sarah.

"We'll have to travel further for water," said Papa.

"Think about it, Jacob," said Matthew. "It will be a three-day trip, maybe four. When we get back home, then what? Water for the crops? There *are no* crops."

Papa looked at Matthew, then away over the land.

Matthew sighed.

"Maggie and I have been talking about another way," he said.

"What?" asked Sarah.

"I think that what Matthew means is

that they're thinking about leaving," said Papa softly.

Sarah turned and looked up at Maggie in the wagon.

"Leaving?" she said, her voice rough and dry like the fields.

Maggie climbed down and went behind the wagon, Sarah following her. I walked closer and stood out of sight, and saw Sarah put out her hand to touch Maggie. But Maggie took a step away, as if Sarah's comfort was too hard. And I heard words I wish I hadn't heard.

"I hate this land!" said Sarah. "I don't have to love it the way Matthew and Jacob love it. They give it everything. Everything! And it gives nothing back."

"They don't know anywhere else, Sarah," said Maggie.

I closed my eyes, but I couldn't close out Sarah's words.

"Jacob once said his name was written in this land, but mine isn't. It isn't!" said Sarah angrily.

"You are like the prairie lark, you know," said Maggie. "It sings its song above the land to let all the birds know it's there before it plunges down to earth to make its home. But you have not come to earth, Sarah."

There was silence then, and I opened my eyes again.

"You don't have to love this land," said Maggie. "But if you don't love it, you won't survive. Jacob's right. You have to write your name in the land to live here."

Sarah didn't speak. She took a handful of dry prairie grass in her hands, letting it crumble through her fingers. Then she walked away from us, through the dried grass, out onto the brown prairie that stretched all the way to the sky. She stood there all alone until Papa went to tell her it was time to go home.

We hung wildflowers from the ceiling to dry them for winter, I remember. Sarah cut our hair, tossing it into the fields so the birds could use it for nests.

And we sang.

When Sarah read books with us, even her words were like a song.

CHAPTER EIGHT

Sarah and I sat in the kitchen. The air was thick with the heat, and there was no breeze. There hadn't been any wind for days. Sarah was writing a letter to the aunts in Maine. I wrote in my journal.

"Remember the wildflowers?" I asked Sarah. "And the roses that grew on the fence? Remember singing?"

Sarah looked up.

"Yes," she said. She reached out and touched my hair. "I remember."

"Papa! Papa! Coyote!" shouted Caleb from outside.

Sarah and I ran outside. By the paddock fence a thin coyote was drinking water out of the water pail.

"He'll kill Moonbeam!" shouted Caleb.

Papa came from the field, took a step toward the coyote, then turned and ran to the house. He came out with his rifle.

"Jacob! What are you going to do?" cried Sarah.

"Go inside, Sarah," he said.

Papa raised his rifle to shoot the coyote, but Sarah grabbed the barrel of the rifle.

"No! Don't do it, Jacob. Don't!

"Sarah! Stop!" yelled Papa.

Papa tried to push her away, and the coyote looked up at the sound of their voices. Slowly he ran away over the fields, stopping once to look back. Then he was gone.

Sarah began to cry.

"He only wanted water. Water, Jacob!"

Tears streamed down her face. Caleb climbed over the paddock fence and stood next to me. Papa took Sarah's arm and turned to Caleb.

"Put the animals in the barn, Caleb," he said.

Caleb turned and walked to the barn.

Sarah began to sob.

"Water!" she said. "He only wanted water. Just like us..."

She slumped to the ground and put her hands over her face as she cried.

"Get Sarah something to drink, Anna," said Papa.

He took off his hat and sat down on the ground next to her.

"Anna," he said sharply. "Now!"

I turned and went to the water barrel and scooped out a cup of water. Papa put his arms around Sarah.

His voice was soft.

"Sarah. Sarah," he said softly. "It will be all right. It will be all right."

But Sarah cried and cried. And when Papa turned and looked at me, I knew that nothing was all right.

The look in his eyes was fear.

And that night, when I came in from the barn to go to bed, there was something else missing from the fence. Missing like Sarah's roses. Caleb's glass was gone.

"They're coming!" said Caleb at the upstairs window.

He wore a clean shirt, and his hair was brushed smooth. I wore the dress I had worn when Papa and Sarah were married. Outside, wagons came into the yard.

"Will this make Sarah happy?" Caleb

asked me, worried.

I watched more wagons drive in. I saw Maggie dressed in a rose dress and a straw hat.

"Yes," I said. "This will make Sarah happy."

"Anna? Caleb? What is this?" said Sarah in the bedroom doorway.

We whirled around, silent. Sarah walked to the window to look out, too, but I took her hand and pulled her out into the hallway. Papa looked up the stairs at her. He wore a waistcoat and his hair was slicked back. He smiled at her.

"Happy birthday, Sarah," he said.

"There are guests. And presents, Sarah!" said Caleb.

"But I'm not dressed," said Sarah.

"Then get dressed," said Papa softly.

Outside there was a table in the shade of the house, set with food and lemonade. Maggie and Matthew were there, and Rose and Violet and the baby. All the neighbours were there, too. Papa carried something covered with a cloth out to the table.

"What is it?" asked Maggie.

"You'll see," said Papa.

"Here she is!" someone said.

We all turned, and Sarah came out on the porch in her white dress.

"Happy birthday, Sarah," said Papa.

"Happy birthday!" everyone called.

Sarah smiled at the sight of them, everyone washed and clean as if the prairie winds had stopped covering us all with dust.

"A present from the aunts," said Papa.

He took the cloth away, and there was a phonograph. I handed him a record and he put the needle on it. Suddenly, music filled the yard. Sarah stared. Papa walked up to her and held out his hand. She smiled and came down the steps and they began to dance. Maggie and Matthew began to dance, too, the baby between them. Everyone danced, then, in the dirt yard, the light around them all yellow like an old photograph. Sarah buried her face in Papa's shoulder, and Caleb smiled at me. And for a little while, as the sun began to set, as they danced, everyone forgot about the drought. For a while, everyone was happy again. Even Sarah. Even Papa.

* * *

The last of the wagons left in the moonlight. Sarah and Papa waved good-bye. Caleb was asleep under the table and Papa took him off to bed. Then Papa helped Sarah carry the phonograph inside.

"I have a present for you, Sarah," I said. I handed her a small book.

"Anna, what is this?" said Sarah.

"It's a book I started. About you. About our family," I said.

Sarah sat down and opened the book. She began to read.

"'When my mother…'"

She stopped and looked at me. I smiled at her, and she began to read again. Papa stood outside the screen door, listening.

"'When my mother, Sarah, came, she came by train. I didn't know I'd love her, but Caleb knew he would. Papa didn't know, either, but he does love her. I have seen them kiss.'" Sarah smiled at me. "'And I have seen the way he looks at her and the way he touches her hair. My mother, Sarah, doesn't love the prairie. She tries, but she can't help remembering what she knew first.'"

Sarah stopped and closed the book,

holding it close to her.

"You like it," I said.

"I like it," said Sarah softly.

She put her arms around me, and I saw Papa watching us.

Sarah got up, then, and went to the door.

"It was a fine party, Jacob."

She put her hand up and he did, too, so that they touched through the screen.

"I'd almost forgotten music," whispered Sarah.

Then she looked past Papa at the fence post.

"Where's Caleb's glass, Jacob?"

Papa didn't speak.

"Put it back, please, Jacob," said Sarah. "It should be there when it rains."

Papa stared at Sarah. And when I went to bed later that night, I looked out and saw it there, shining and clean, on the fence post.

CHAPTER NINE

The next day, after the party, after the music and dancing, Matthew and Maggie's well went dry. They drove their wagon to our house to say good-bye, and I could hardly look at Sarah's face.

The wagon was packed with furniture and clothes; Rose and Violet sat in the back, the baby on Maggie's lap.

"I'm sorry to be leaving you, Jacob," said Matthew.

"It's all right, Matthew. I know," said Papa.

"I'll miss you," Sarah said to Maggie. Her face was tight, as if she had to keep all her feelings from coming out. She reached out to touch the baby's hand.

"We'll be back," said Maggie.

Tears came down her face.

"We'll be back," she repeated.

The baby began to cry as the wagon

drove out of the yard. When Sarah turned to look at Papa, tears sat at the corners of her eyes.

"They'll be back," said Papa.

He watched the cloud of dust that followed Matthew's wagon down the road, his eyes narrowed against the sunlight.

That night I dreamed about roses, and green fields, and water. A glass of water on the fence post, and ponds of water to swim in; Caleb spitting streams of water in the air like a whale. Sarah laughing and splashing us with water.

A sharp clap of thunder woke me. Lottie and Nick barked as lightning lit up the sky. I turned over in bed, but then Papa's voice from downstairs made me sit up.

"Sarah! Sarah! It's fire!"

I got up and rushed to the window, and there was fire in the field close to the barn. Flames creeping up the fence, flames near the corral.

I ran downstairs and out to the porch, Caleb behind me. Sarah, in her nightgown, her hair down her back, ran with wet

sacks. And Sarah and Papa beat the flames around the corral. Papa stopped to let the frightened horses out.

"Get the cows," he shouted to Sarah.

Sarah ran to the barn and pulled the cows outside.

"Shoo! Shoo!" she cried. Caleb ran down to get Moonbeam.

"Get on the porch and stay there," Sarah shouted at him as he led Moonbeam away.

I put my arm around Caleb. I could feel him trembling.

Sarah screamed as some hay caught fire and the side of the barn burst into flame.

"Buckets!" shouted Papa. "Get buckets of water! Buckets!"

Sarah ran to the barrel and filled a bucket, running back to him as the fire grew. Papa grabbed it and then Sarah stopped him. I couldn't hear what she said, but I knew what it was. It was the last barrel. Papa stopped, then, and stared at the barn as flames caught the dry wood and then the roof. Sparks flew everywhere. And then part of the roof fell and Sarah and Papa moved back. Sarah put her arm around Papa as the barn burned. They stood there watching for a long time. Papa turned once to look away from the fire and I could see his eyes, shining red from the fire.

I have never seen Papa's face so sad.

The sun came up in the morning the way it always did. But everything had changed. The barn was gone, only a few blackened timbers standing. The cows walked in the yard, the sheep in the cornfield, looking for green grass. I stood at my window and watched Sarah and Papa talking by the clothesline. I saw her shake her head, no. I saw Papa take her hand. She shook her head again. Then Papa put his arms around her.

I knew we would have to go away.

They told us at dinnertime.

"Maine?" said Caleb. "Are you coming, too, Papa?"

Papa shook his head and looked at Sarah.

"I have to stay here," he said softly. "I can't go away from the land."

"Can Seal and the dogs come?" Caleb asked.

Papa shook his head.

"They'll be happier here," he said. "I'll take care of them."

"What will you do while we're gone, Papa?" asked Caleb.

"I'll miss you," Papa said softly, reaching out to take Caleb's hand. He looked at me, then, and as if he knew I would cry if I spoke, he took my hand, too.

"What will happen to us?" I asked after a moment.

Papa looked at Sarah, and his words were for her.

"We will write letters," he said, his voice soft. "We've written letters before, you know."

CHAPTER TEN

We travelled three days and nights on the train across the dry prairies. We passed packed wagons. We passed through towns and cities. We slept to the clackety sound of the train and woke with the red sun. Caleb was excited, looking out of the window. Sarah was tired and sad. Sometimes I read to her from my journal.

"'When Sarah came, she wore a yellow bonnet,'" I read. "'She brought Seal to us. The corn was high and the wheat all yellow. We lay down with the sheep in the fields, and Sarah taught us how to swim.'"

"'When they were married, my mother, Sarah, wore a dress soft like mist, and a veil. And Papa cried...'"

Sarah turned to me. "Did he?" she asked, her voice soft. "Did he cry?"

I smiled and Sarah closed her eyes. I

covered her with a shawl.

We went over a bridge, the river shining in the sun.

Caleb turned from the window. "Sarah?"

Sarah opened her eyes.

"Is this the way you came?" he asked.

Sarah looked out at the land. "Yes, Caleb," she said softly. "This is the way I came."

Maine was green. When we got off the train, Sarah stood still. She looked at the train station, and at the trees, and the people.

"Sarah?" I said.

"It's all right, Anna," said Sarah. "It's just what you wrote in your book. I've come back to what I knew first."

"Sarah! Sarah Wheaton!"

A man waved to Sarah. He wore a waistcoat and a gold chain across it.

Sarah smiled.

"Chub!" she said. "You're still here!"

The man hugged Sarah.

"Where would I be?" he said. "Except dead, maybe. Are the hens meeting you?"

Sarah laughed.

"No. And I'm Sarah Witting now. These are my children, Anna and Caleb. Can you take us there?"

"Get in."

We got in Chub's car, open all around, with shining brass trim and wood on the side.

"I've never been in a car before," whispered Caleb.

"It's about time you were," said Chub. "Want to drive?"

"No," said Caleb, looking around. Then he smiled at Chub. "I won't tell the aunts you call them hens, either."

Chub laughed. He started the car. We passed green grass and green trees and flowers blooming in green gardens as we drove to the house where Sarah had lived.

And then we saw the sea.

"All that water!" said Caleb, running down the lawn of the aunts' house. Sarah and I looked out over the water: at the cliffs that went down to the sea; at birds that flew over us; at boats with white sails like clouds.

"Come on," said Sarah after a moment. She took our hands. "Let's go

meet the aunts."

We walked up the lawn to the house. The house was tall and big with shutters on the windows. There were gardens with flowers I had never seen before.

"Will they like us?" asked Caleb.

"They will love you," said Sarah, laughing. "They will fall upon you with kisses."

We walked up the steps of the big porch. Sarah put out her hand to open the door, but it swung open, and a woman in a silk dress stood there, her feet bare. Her eyes widened when she saw us. Her hand went up to her mouth. Sarah smiled.

"Hello, Mattie," she said softly. "We're home."

The aunts laughed and cried and fed us.

"I loved your letters," said Aunt Mattie. "I loved all the pictures you drew." She kissed Sarah and Caleb and she kissed me. Then she kissed Sarah again.

Aunt Harriet, tall with wire glasses, in bare feet, too, tried to feed us all the food in the kitchen.

"I made these cookies, Anna, Caleb," she said. "Are you tired? I made the bread too. And the soup! Do you want a nap? Do you want a bath?"

"Harriet, let them be!" said Aunt Mattie.

Sarah leaned over close to us.

"See?" she said. "I told you."

And then Aunt Lou, dressed in overalls and high boots, came in the front door with her dog.

"Lou!" said Sarah.

Aunt Lou hugged Sarah. She hugged me.

"Mind that beast," said Aunt Harriet.

"The beast's name is Brutus," said Aunt Lou.

"Lou works with animals," said Aunt Harriet.

"Lou works with a veterinarian," said Aunt Lou. She kissed Caleb twice. "Harriet wants me in silk and pearls."

Brutus jumped up on Caleb's lap.

"Oh, get away!" scolded Aunt Harriet.

"Dogs like me," said Caleb, smiling. "We have two dogs at home."

"This is what we've needed all along, a child!" said Aunt Lou, hugging Caleb.

"We must get ourselves one."

"It looks like we have two," said Aunt Mattie softly.

"Sarah," said Aunt Harriet, "will Jacob be coming, too?"

Sarah looked out the window.

"No," she said softly. "Jacob won't be coming."

"Papa's home," I said.

Somehow hearing my own words made it worse. I started to cry. Sarah put her arms around me, and I cried harder.

"Papa had to stay home."

Maine is green and full of voices and people laughing and talking, the tide going in and going out, the moon rising above the water. Sarah loves it here. The last thing every night she walks by the water, and the first thing in the morning she is there, too. Now I know how much she missed her old home. I miss my home. I miss Lottie and Nick and the land and the big sky.

I miss Papa.

CHAPTER ELEVEN

It took longer for Caleb to miss Papa. Caleb swam every day in the cold water. Aunt Lou wrapped him in blankets when he came out, shivering, his teeth chattering. He went fishing with Lou and with Sarah's brother, William, who was so happy when he first saw Sarah that he ran up the hill and whirled her around in his arms. It made me think of Papa and Sarah turning around and around in the prairie wind at night.

William's wife, Meg, hugged Sarah too.

"Over a year!" she said. "It's been ages since we've seen you!"

Over a year. I looked at Sarah and wondered if she was thinking what I was thinking. Would it be more than a year before we saw Papa?

"William looks like you, Sarah," said Caleb.

"Plain and tall, I told you so," said Sarah. "Remember?"

"Did you hear what I just heard?" said Aunt Harriet as we picnicked on a blanket in the grass by the sea. "Seal is going to have kittens!"

"The father is orange," called Caleb, making the aunts laugh.

"Seal!" exclaimed William. "I remember that Seal was independent. Independent like Sarah."

William put his arm around Sarah. The sun came out from a cloud, but it wasn't hot like home. It was cool and green and beautiful. But it didn't make me happy. I thought about Papa at home by himself, building the barn in the hot sun.

"Where was your dune, Sarah?" asked Caleb.

"Down there," said Sarah, pointing to an inlet.

"I remember when Papa made us a dune," said Caleb softly. He looked up at Sarah. "A dune made of hay. Do you remember?"

"Yes," said Sarah. "I remember, Caleb."

Sarah looked over at me as the aunts

talked and laughed. She reached out to touch my arm.

"It's all right, Anna," she said softly. "It's all right."

But it wasn't.

The next week letters came from Papa. Sarah, Caleb, William, and I rowed out in the bay in William's rowboat, and Caleb read his letter.

"'Dear Caleb, Moonbeam is getting bigger every day. I have started building the barn. Still no rain, but yesterday Seal had four kittens!'"

"Four!" said William. Sarah smiled.

"'Three are grey like Seal,'" Caleb read. "'One is orange. Nick and Lottie miss you. Every day they sit looking down the road, waiting for you to come home. I love you. Give Sarah a kiss from me. Love, Papa.'"

William rowed to shore, and we pulled the boat up.

"Papa misses us, too," I said to Sarah. "When he writes about Nick and Lottie waiting for us. Remember you once said that Papa's letters were full of things between the lines?"

"Yes," said Sarah.

I leaned over and kissed her.

"That's Papa's kiss," I said.

William leaned over to kiss Sarah, too.

"And that's mine," he said.

Dear Anna,

It is quiet here without you. I miss your voices and Sarah's songs. Sometimes, if I close my eyes, I think I can hear them.

Love,

Papa

The aunts played music. Harriet played a flute that squeaked sometimes. Aunt Lou played the piano in bare feet, and Brutus watched her pedal. Aunt Mattie danced with a long scarf and a serious look that made Caleb laugh.

Sarah took naps in the afternoons and slept late in the mornings.

Chub drove Sarah away and back again one afternoon. Aunt Lou said she had gone to the doctor.

"Are you sick, Sarah?" I asked her that night.

She smiled at me, a small smile at first,

then a big smile.

"No, Anna. I'm not sick."

She was in bed, her long hair down.

"Read me your Papa's letters again," she said.

When I did, she smiled more.

"Sarah?"

We looked up. Caleb stood in the door. He was in his pyjamas, his hair all messed from sleep.

"Caleb, what's the matter?" asked Sarah.

"A dream I had," he said softly. "A dream about Papa."

"That's a good dream," said Sarah.

She lifted the covers and Caleb got into bed with her.

"I dreamed that Papa looked and looked and couldn't find us," said Caleb.

"Oh, Caleb," said Sarah, putting her arm around him. "Your Papa knows where we are. He does."

Caleb picked up the family picture that Sarah kept on her bed stand.

"I used to dream about rain, remember?" he said.

Sarah nodded.

"Now I dream about Papa."

There was silence in the room and then Caleb looked at Sarah.

"Is this our new home, Sarah?" he asked softly.

Sarah didn't answer. She put her arms around him and looked at me over his head. She began to sing very softly.

"Hush little baby,
Don't say a word.
Papa's going to buy you
A mocking bird."

I thought of Joshua, the photographer, who had told us about his grandfather leaving the prairie.

"Did he come back?" Caleb had asked him.

No, he never came back.

And that night I dreamed Caleb's dream: Papa looking for us. He could hear Sarah's song and our voices, and he searched the fields and the house and the barn. But we weren't there.

Chapter Twelve

We woke to a new sound. A sound I hadn't heard for months. I ran to the window. Rain.

"Anna!"

I turned, and Caleb and I grinned at each other. We dressed quickly and ran downstairs to the porch. Rain came down, filling the rain gutters. It sent little rivers down the driveway. Everything smelled sweet. Caleb spread his arms and ran out into the rain in his clothes, racing around the yard. I laughed and ran after him. We jumped and ran, feeling the cool water run down our faces. We looked up, and Sarah stood on the porch. She smiled, and, very slowly, she walked down the steps and lifted her face to the rain. Then she ran down the lawn to take our hands and dance with us. The aunts came out on the porch to watch.

"Rain!" Sarah called to them. "It's been so long!"

William came up from the water in his yellow mackintosh and hat to watch, too. Then, laughing, he took off his mackintosh to dance with us until the aunts made us come up and dry off with towels. We were sorry to see the sun come out.

"I remember you when you were little," William said to Sarah. "Running, climbing. You were always in the trees; out on the rocks. You never stayed still."

Suddenly Sarah looked at William.

"Do you remember a song Papa used to sing about a skylark?" she asked.

William smiled.

"A poem. I only remember the first line: 'Like a skylark Sarah sings!' Papa said you'd never come to earth."

Sarah looked out over the sea, and I knew she was thinking of Maggie's words to her on the dry prairie. Words I wasn't supposed to hear. "You're like the prairie lark, Sarah...you'll never come to earth."

That night I wrote Papa a letter.

Dear Papa,

Caleb and I miss you. Sarah misses you, too. We are fine. We went fishing and rowing in William's boat. Sometimes seals poke their heads out of the water to watch us. You would love the sea.

Write soon,

Love, Anna.

PS I gave Sarah your kiss.

I didn't tell Papa about the rain.

The aunts had tea in the moonlight. The light lay like a blanket over the water below.

"Have you ever been married, Aunt Harriet?" asked Caleb.

"Caleb! That's private," I said.

But Aunt Harriet smiled. She took Caleb on her lap.

"Private, maybe," she said. "But like everything else, it's history. No, I was never married. Almost, but not quite. I never met a dashing man like your father."

"What's dashing?" asked Caleb.

"That's what I'm doing," said Aunt Lou, coming down the path. She was dressed in a bathrobe. "I'm dashing into the water. Do you want to come? I'm going skinny-dipping."

"Do you mean you're going to swim all naked?" asked Caleb.

Caleb followed Aunt Lou down the path. And then his voice came up the hill.

"Anna! Come here! In the moonlight she looks like a big fish!"

Aunt Harriet and Aunt Mattie laughed, Aunt Mattie so hard she spilled her tea. And then it was quiet again.

"Everyone goes skinny-dipping," said Sarah. Her voice was soft with memory.

I thought about the pond at home when the moon came up so big and close it seemed you could touch it. Far off a loon cried on the water. The bell buoy made a lonely, sad sound.

That night, under the same moon that Papa saw, we could see fireworks from the faraway town. Splashes of colour in the sky, red and silver and green.

"They're like the dandelions that bloom in the fields at home in summer," I told Sarah.

Sarah reached over and took my hand.

"Do you think the drought's over yet?" asked Caleb, leaning against Sarah.

"No," said Sarah. "It's not over, Caleb. It may be a long time."

Her voice was low, her eyes dark and sad. She looked at me.

A long time. I didn't like those words, *a long time*.

CHAPTER THIRTEEN

More letters came from Papa. The dogs missed us. *Papa missed us.* All our days were long days filled with green all around us, and the sea. The rain should have made us happy, but it didn't. It made us think about Papa. Even Caleb looked sad now. One day Sarah showed him the woolly ragwort that grew in Maine, but it didn't make Caleb laugh the way it used to.

At night Caleb had bad dreams. I could hear him, and I could hear Sarah singing him back to sleep.

Sarah wrote letters to Papa every day. At night she read his letters over and over again, the light from the oil lamp spilling into the hallway.

Dear Anna and Caleb and Sarah,

Somehow it isn't so hot now. The nights are cooler and the dogs are sleeping in my room again. Sometimes Lottie tries to climb up on my bed.

I love you all.

Jacob

And then, one day at dinner, Caleb said something that made my heart skip a beat.

"It's almost time for school," he said.

Fall was almost here, the air cool and crisp in the mornings as if frost would come soon. I had hardly thought about fall and school. My thoughts were about summer, and Papa, and the sweet smell of the prairie grass.

The aunts looked at Sarah, then at Caleb and me.

"Would you like to visit the school here, Caleb?" said Aunt Harriet.

"It's a wonderful school, Caleb," said Sarah slowly. She sighed. "I went to school there."

Caleb stood up and looked at us. Very carefully he pushed in his chair.

"No," he said. "I don't want to go to school here. I like you, but I don't want to live here."

Caleb walked to the door, opened it.

"I want to go home," he said in a soft voice. He looked at Sarah. "Don't you?" he asked. "Don't *you* want to go home, Sarah?" Then he left.

It was quiet. I stared at my plate of food. I could feel Aunt Mattie beside me, fiddling with her fork. Harriet cleared her throat. When I looked up again, Sarah was staring out of the window at the sea. No one spoke.

I looked everywhere for Caleb: behind the house, in the wooden rowboat, on the rocks where the seals sunned. I found him huddled by a driftwood log in the cove. Caleb was crying.

I sat down next to him and listened to the waves come in. A wind came up and I put my arms around him.

"Don't cry, Caleb," I said. "Please don't cry."

After a moment Caleb looked up at me. I could see his eyes shining in the moonlight. I thought of Papa's eyes shining when the barn burned.

"Anna," said Caleb, his voice soft, "will

we see Papa again? Ever?"

Caleb waited for me to answer. But I couldn't find any words for him. He began to cry again. And we sat there as the moon moved across the sky.

CHAPTER FOURTEEN

The August sun rose red, then turned gold. It touched the flowers of the aunts' gardens, the beds of late roses and nasturtiums and asters. Geese flew in, sitting calmly on the water. A boat with two masts and a tall sail slipped by. Caleb went fishing with William and came home with two fish.

"Flounder," said William, smiling at us.

But Caleb didn't smile.

In the afternoon we walked by the water, Aunt Lou and Sarah, Caleb and I. Caleb threw sticks for Brutus, who brought them back along with big rocks and seaweed and whatever came up with the tide. We began to walk up the path again, Caleb carrying sticks, Sarah stopping to pick a hatful of rose hips. A fisherman pulled up lobster pots in the cove. Then, suddenly, Caleb straightened and looked past me to the top of the hill. He didn't speak, but his lips moved.

"What?" I asked him, and I turned to see a figure standing there, looking out at the sea.

Caleb's mouth opened and he dropped his sticks.

Papa. I leaned closer to hear him, and then he shouted.

"Papa! Papa!"

He began running up the hill calling Papa's name over and over. And I saw Papa turn at the sound of Caleb's voice. I ran, too, Sarah running behind me, and I began to cry.

"Papa!"

Caleb ran into Papa's arms and Papa held him close. Papa picked me up, too, and my hat fell off, and I buried my face in his neck.

Papa looked at Sarah.

"It rained," he said.

He smiled at her.

"I never thought you'd come," whispered Sarah.

"It rained," Papa said again, his voice

so soft that it could have been the wind I heard.

Caleb sat on Papa's lap.

"And there are fireworks, Papa! Lots of them! How big are the kittens?"

"Big, like you," said Papa, smiling. He reached out and touched Caleb's face.

"Restless, like you."

"Do you want something to eat, Jacob?" asked Aunt Harriet.

"Harriet's solution to the problems of the world," said Aunt Lou, making Papa smile.

"No, thank you," said Papa. "I couldn't eat."

He stood, looking out over the water. No one spoke.

"*That sound,*" Papa whispered after a moment.

"The sea," said Sarah.

Papa turned to look at her. She touched his arm and walked off down the path to the water. Papa looked down at Caleb and me quickly; then he followed her.

Caleb started to walk after Papa, but I reached out and took his hand.

"Caleb," I said softly.
"Where are they going?" Caleb asked.
"They'll come back," I said. "It's all right, Caleb."
Caleb and I stood and watched Sarah and Papa walk down the hill. They stopped. They talked. And then, after a moment, Papa put his arms around Sarah. I smiled.
"It's all right," I whispered to Caleb.

That night, after Aunt Harriet and Aunt Lou had played music for Papa, and Mattie had danced, we walked down by the water. Clouds passed over the full moon. And then Sarah and Papa told us that in the spring we would have a new baby.
"A real baby?" asked Caleb, excited.
"A real baby," said Papa.
"*Our* baby!" said Caleb, smiling.
Sarah saw my face and she knew I was worried. Worried because Mama had died when Caleb was born.
"It will be fine," she told me. "I am healthy. The baby's healthy. The doctor said so."
I looked at Papa.

"It will be fine, Anna," he said.

The clouds passed, and the moon spread out over the water.

Papa put his arms around me.

"And it will be *wonderful*," he said.

CHAPTER FIFTEEN

"I see the house!" cried Caleb, standing up in the wagon. "And the new barn!"

The wagon passed the cornfields, still dry, but we could see some green in the meadow. We turned into our yard, and Nick and Lottie ran and jumped up into the wagon before it stopped.

"Nick, Lottie!"

I laughed as they jumped on us, licking our faces.

"There's some water in the pond," said Papa. He looked at Caleb and me. "And there are kittens waiting for you on the porch."

Caleb and I ran to the porch, where Seal washed her four kittens, three gray and one orange like Maggie's cat, Sam.

"Look, Sarah!" Caleb held the orange cat for Sarah to see. She smiled at us, and then she and Papa began to walk out to the fields to see the green. I watched them, Papa dressed in his wedding suit, Sarah in her yellow bonnet. And then Sarah bent down suddenly, her travelling coat spread out behind her. She picked up a stick and began to write in the dry earth.

"What is she doing?" asked Caleb.

I knew, but I didn't say anything.

Papa turned and walked back to her, looking down at what she had written. She smiled up at him, and the two of them walked out into the fields in the late pale light of afternoon. Papa reached out and took Sarah's hand.

Caleb and I walked down the steps. Under the post where Caleb's glass still stood, Sarah had written one name in the prairie dirt.

Sarah.

Home—

It has rained twice. But there is still dust. The corn still rattles in the wind.

The green of Maine seems to be only a dream. When we came home by train, we passed trees and hills and lakes filled with water. They are beautiful, the trees and hills and lakes filled with water. But the prairie is home, the sky so big it takes your breath away, the land like a giant quilt tossed out.

It will rain again. There is some water in the pond. Not enough for swimming, but there will be. There will be flowers in the spring, and the river will run again. And in the spring there will be the new baby, Papa and Sarah's baby.

Caleb, like Papa, is not always good with words. But I think Caleb says it best.

Our baby.

Journey to Jo'Burg
by Beverley Naidoo £2.50

Naledi had made up her mind. Dineo was ill and needed Mother, but she worked and lived three hundred miles away in Johannesburg. The only way to let her know was to get to the big road and walk. So Naledi and her brother Tiro did just that. Their journey illustrates at every turn the grim realities of apartheid – the pass laws, the bantustans, the racism, and the breakdown of family life.

Chain of Fire
by Beverley Naidoo £2.99

When the villagers of Bophelong discover that they are to be forcibly evicted from their houses and sent to a barren piece of land designated by the apartheid government of South Africa as their "homeland", they decide to resist. But will their protests work, or will apartheid crush them? Or are they all links in a chain of resistance which is each day lengthening and strengthening? *Chain of Fire* is an impassioned and provocative story of struggle.

Order Form

To order direct from the publishers, just make a list of the titles you want and fill in the form below:

Name ....

Address ....

....

....

Send to: Dept 6, HarperCollins Publishers Ltd, Westerhill Road, Bishopbriggs, Glasgow G64 2QT.

Please enclose a cheque or postal order to the value of the cover price, plus:

UK & BFPO: Add £1.00 for the first book, and 25p per copy for each addition book ordered.

Overseas and Eire: Add £2.95 service charge. Books will be sent by surface mail but quotes for airmail despatch will be given on request.

A 24-hour telephone ordering service is avail-able to Visa and Access card holders: 041-772 2281